KT-528-918

To Sheila

Text and illustrations copyright © 1993 Peter Utton

First published in Great Britain in 1993 by **ABC**

This edition first published in 1993 by softbacks,
an imprint of **ABC** , All Books for Children,
a division of The All Children's Company Ltd
33 Museum Street, London WC1A 1LD

Printed and bound in Hong Kong

British Library Cataloguing in Publication Data
Utton, Peter
What if . . .
I. Title
823

ISBN 1-85704-035-X

173139

This is

................................'s

book

What if . . .

Peter Utton

FALKIRK COUNCIL
LIBRARY SUPPORT
FOR SCHOOLS

softbacks

What if . . . just as the wounded
soldier climbs up the last jagged bit
of mountain, he sees, through
the mists of time, the door
to a warm and
cosy cave . . .

But what if . . .

. . . just as he reaches the door to the
warm and cosy cave, he sees . . .

. . . a hideous, smelly .
monster from outer
space who has got
there first and is
about to drink
his milk!

But what if, just at that moment, a space cleaning machine comes and sucks up the monster and rushes it off to a hideous, smelly planet where it can be hideous, smelly and happy.

Phew! That was close!
But what if . . .

. . . someone has left open the door
to the secret tunnel . . .

. . . and the secret tunnel has been discovered by a band of bloodthirsty pirates searching for treasure!

Phew! That was close!
But what if . . .

. . . that isn't really his
baby sister asleep in
her crib . . .

. . . but is a giant-hairy-octopus-spider waiting to ambush innocent travellers . . .

But
what if . . .

. . . just in the nick of time, a giant-hairy-octopus-spider-eating-bird (who's on our side) swoops down and drags the giant-hairy-octopus-spider off for its supper!

Phew! That was close!

But what if . . . the bedroom door
should suddenly start to open . . .

. . . but it's only Pegasus his trusty wonder horse,

who's come to rescue his lord
and master!

FALKIRK COUNCIL
LIBRARY SUPPORT
FOR SCHOOLS

Phew! That was close!